It's a Field Trip, Busy Bus!

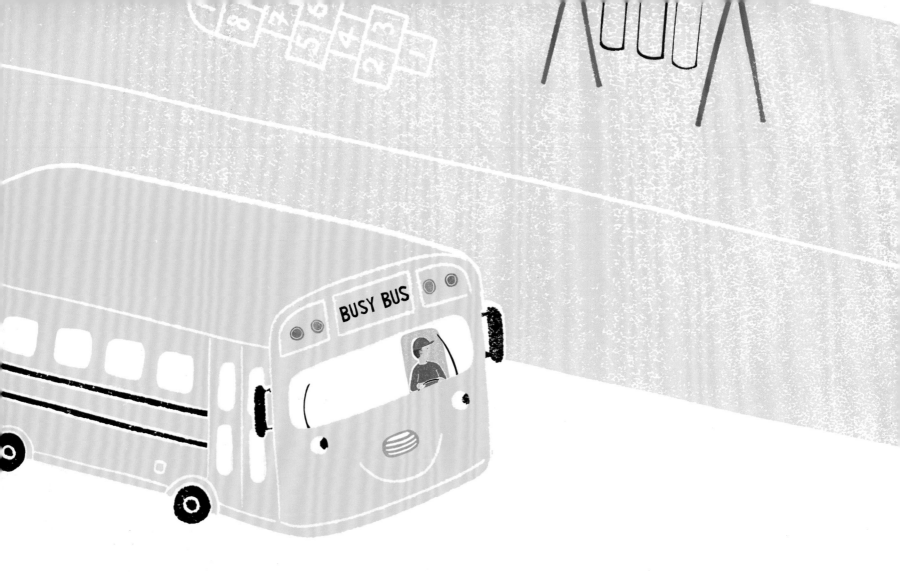

BUSY BUS

It's a Field Trip,

written by
Jody Jensen Shaffer

illustrated by
Claire Messer

Busy Bus!

BEACH LANE BOOKS · New York   London   Toronto   Sydney   New Delhi

"Today is a special day," says Ben the bus driver. "It's your first field trip, Busy Bus!"

HONK!

BUSY BUS

STOP

Busy Bus can't wait.
He and the children are going
to meet a fire truck!

"Welcome to the fire station!" says the captain.
"Let's meet Engine 4."

Engine 4 is red.
Engine 4 is shiny.
Engine 4 is huge.

"Engine 4 is a fire-fighting beast!" says the captain.
"It saves people and their things."

The children *love* Engine 4.

Suddenly Busy Bus feels very small.

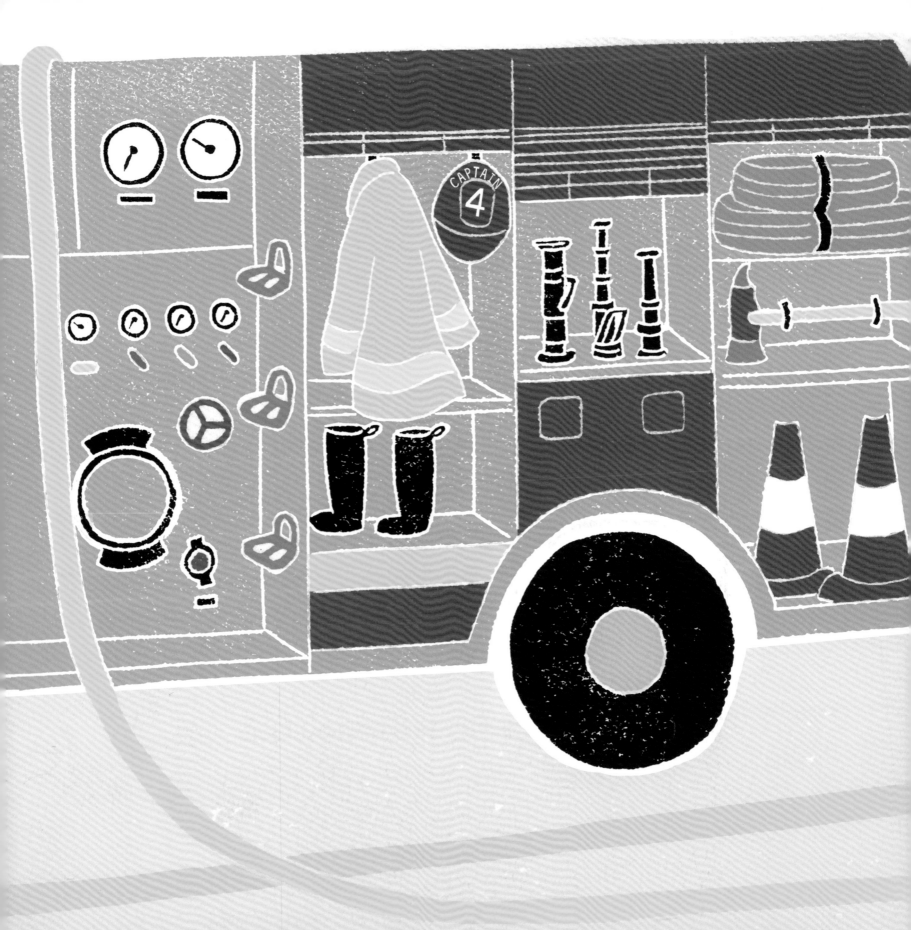

The captain lifts Engine 4's sliding doors. *Zip!* "These are hoses," she says. "Water runs through them so firefighters can put out fires."

ZIP!

WHOOSH!

I wish I could put out fires, thinks Busy Bus.

"Sometimes there are fires in tall buildings," says the captain.
"Firefighters use Engine 4's ladder to reach them."

Engine 4's ladder goes

UP

UP

UP

Busy Bus can hardly see the top.

I wish I had a ladder, he thinks.

"Engine 4 rushes to emergencies. So firefighters use a siren to warn people they're coming. Cover your ears, everyone," says the captain.

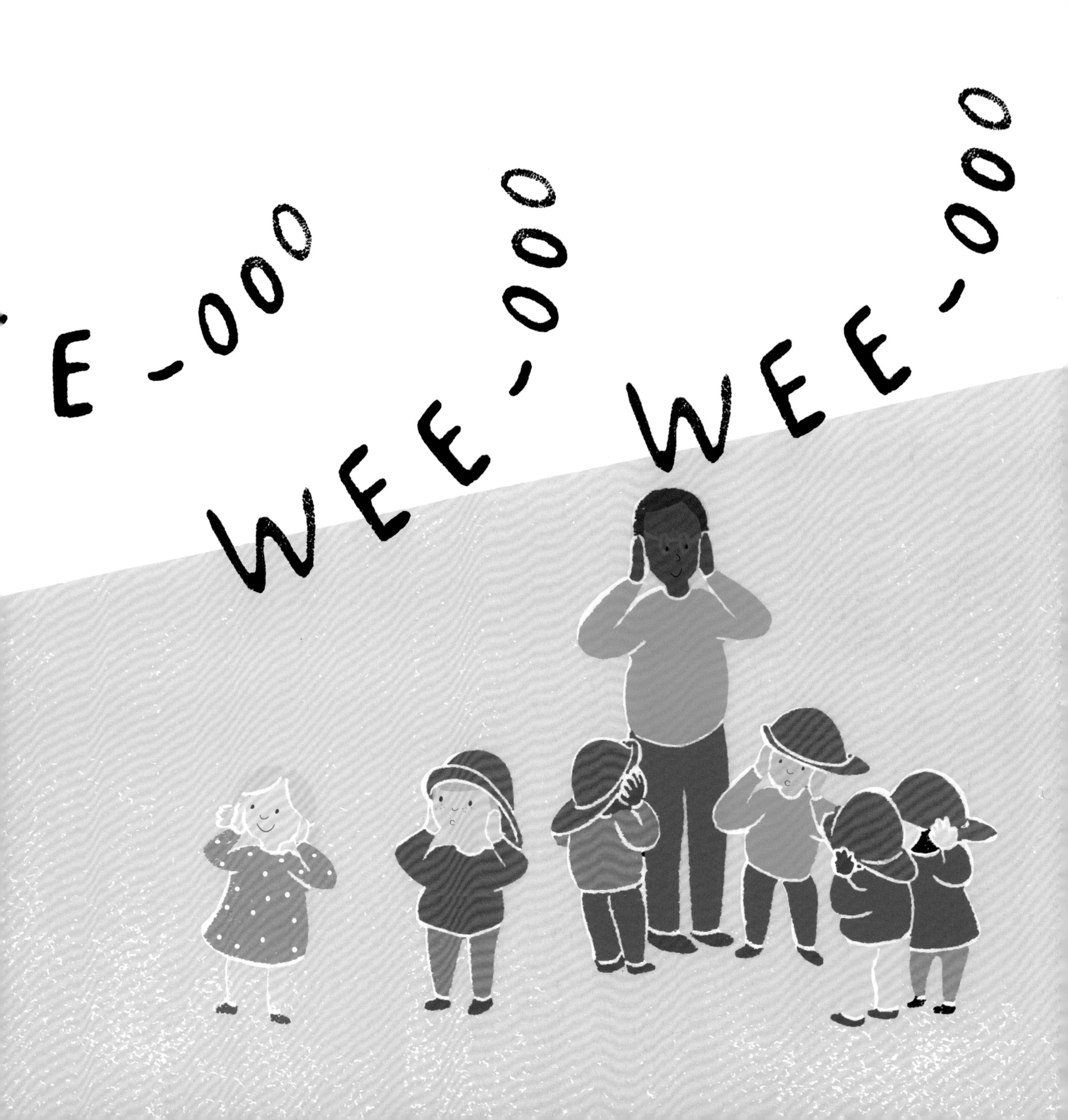
E-OOO
WEE-OOO
WEE-OOO

Busy Bus's wipers sag.

I can't put out fires.

I can't reach tall buildings.

And the only sound I make is a honk, Busy Bus thinks.

Will the children still like me?

Then the captain says, "Engine 4 is an amazing vehicle. But it can't do everything."

Really? thinks Busy Bus.

"Engine 4 doesn't have a stop arm so children can get on and off safely," says the captain.

But I do, thinks Busy Bus.

"Engine 4 can't carry children
to and from school each day."

But I can, thinks Busy Bus.

"And Engine 4 can't take children on field trips to learn about community helpers," says the captain.

FIRE STATION 4

HONK!

But I can, thinks Busy Bus.
And I just did!

"Hooray for Busy Bus!" cheer the children.

Hooray for field trips and friends! thinks Busy Bus.
Where will we go next?

For Tom,
beside me on the ride—J. J. S.

For the "Beach House,"
Station 2, Santa Monica—C. M.

BEACH LANE BOOKS

An imprint of Simon & Schuster Children's Publishing Division • 1230 Avenue of the Americas, New York, New York 10020 • Text copyright © 2019 by
Jody Jensen Shaffer • Illustrations copyright © 2019 by Claire Messer • All rights reserved, including the right of reproduction in whole or in part in
any form. • BEACH LANE BOOKS is a trademark of Simon & Schuster, Inc. • For information about special discounts for bulk purchases, please contact
Simon & Schuster Special Sales at 1-866-506-1949 or business@simonandschuster.com. • The Simon & Schuster Speakers Bureau can bring authors to
your live event. For more information or to book an event, contact the Simon & Schuster Speakers Bureau at 1-866-248-3049 or visit our website at
www.simonspeakers.com. • Book design by Lauren Rille • The text for this book was set in Lunchbox. • The illustrations for this book were rendered in
lino prints and black-and-white ink and then colored digitally. • Manufactured in China • 0619 SCP • First Edition • 10 9 8 7 6 5 4 3 2 1 •
Library of Congress Cataloging-in-Publication Data • Names: Shaffer, Jody Jensen, author. | Messer, Claire, illustrator. • It's a field trip, Busy Bus! / Jody
Jensen Shaffer ; illustrated by Claire Messer. • Other titles: It is a field trip, Busy Bus! • First edition. | New York : Beach Lane Books, [2019] | Summary:
Busy Bus is excited to take the children on a field trip to the fire station—until he meets Engine 4, who seems bigger and better at everything. • Iden-
tifiers: LCCN 2018039907 | ISBN 9781534440814 (hardcover : alk. paper) ISBN 9781534440821 (eBook) • Subjects: CYAC: School buses—Fiction. | Fire
engines—Fiction. | School field trips—Fiction. | Jealousy—Fiction. • Classification: LCC PZ7.1.S4745 Ip 2019 | DDC [E]dc23 • LC record available at https://
lccn.loc.gov/2018039907